For Rachel and all that she has done to further all the dreams she shared with Jackie,
and for all the Jackies in this world who need a chance
—M. L.

To all the schoolchildren I've had the pleasure of meeting
—B. P.

SIMON & SCHUSTER BOOKS FOR YOUNG READERS
An imprint of Simon & Schuster Children's Publishing Division
1230 Avenue of the Americas, New York, New York 10020
Text copyright © 2006 by Marybeth Lorbiecki
Illustrations copyright © 2006 by Brian Pinkney
All rights reserved, including the right of reproduction in whole or in part in any form.
SIMON & SCHUSTER BOOKS FOR YOUNG READERS is a trademark of Simon & Schuster, Inc.
Book design by Daniel Roode
The text for this book is set in Futura.
The illustrations for this book are rendered in watercolor on paper.
Manufactured in China
2 4 6 8 10 9 7 5 3 1
Library of Congress Cataloging-in-Publication Data
Lorbiecki, Marybeth.
Jackie's bat / by Marybeth Lorbiecki ; illustrated by Brian Pinkney.
p. cm.
Summary: Joey, the batboy for the Brooklyn Dodgers in 1947, learns a hard lesson about respect for
people of different races after Jackie Robinson joins the team.
ISBN-13: 978-0-689-84102-6
ISBN-10: 0-689-84102-7
1. Robinson, Jackie, 1919–1972—Juvenile fiction. [1. Robinson, Jackie, 1919–1972—Fiction.
2. Race relations—Fiction. 3. Baseball—Fiction. 4. Brooklyn Dodgers (Baseball team)—Fiction.]
I. Pinkney, J. Brian, ill. II. Title.
PZ7.L8766 Jac 2006
[Fic]—dc21
2001049353

Special thanks to Rachel Robinson for her encouragement on this project; to agent Edythea Ginis
Selman for her friendship and ongoing support of me and my career; and to Diane Arico for her keen
eye and insightful push for further development. Also thanks to Ken Burns and his wonderful series on
baseball, which launched my research; to Lucy Perez, Julie Dunlap, Jill Andersen, Muriel Dubois, and
Marybeth Nierengarten for their writing and editorial feedback; and to my husband, David, and
children, Nadja, Mirjana, and Dmitri, for their patience and their love of books, writing, and me.
—M. L.

first
edition

JACKIE'S BAT

Marybeth Lorbiecki

illustrated by Brian Pinkney

SIMON & SCHUSTER BOOKS FOR YOUNG READERS
New York • London • Toronto • Sydney

*My pops and me have been going
to baseball games since I was three.*

Our team has always been "dem bums,"
the Brooklyn Dodgers.
They've had their slumps,
but this season—1947—is going to be their best ever,
and you know why?
'Cause I'm their batboy.
It's my first day,
and I get to the locker room
earlier than anyone.

A new player comes in.
I ain't never seen him play,
but I've heard all about him.
He's Jackie Robinson.
He looks around for a locker,
but there aren't any more.
I do what the manager told me
and point to a folding chair and a nail on the wall.
I don't think any other player ever had to start with a nail.
But Robinson ain't like any other player—
not in either of the leagues.
He's colored.
In spring training, a bunch of the guys on the team
said they didn't want to play with him.
But old "Leo the Lion" Durocher
just chewed their rear ends
and said Robinson was staying.
Anyone who didn't like it could leave.
No one did.

I ain't leaving either.

Robinson looks at me.
"Hey kid," he says, all smiles and friendly-like.
I don't know what to say.
Pops says it ain't right,
a white boy serving a black man.
So I turn and get to work.

Then I cart the bats, gloves, and balls
down to the field.

For the first game against the Yanks,
there's a mob of colored fans
waiting for Robinson,
hoping for his autograph.
He hasn't even done anything yet!

"Hey, kid," he says to me. "What's your name?"
"Joey," I say.
"Could you get me a pen?" he asks politely.
But I keep walking, pretending I don't hear.
Before he can ask again, a fan calls out,
"Here, Mr. Robinson, have mine!"
He takes the pen
and seems to forget all about me.

I don't forget about him.
I take care of all the other players,
but I steer clear of Robinson.
I've started to get the hang of my job,
and now I'm as ready as can be
for the opening game against the Braves.

As the players' names are called,
the fans go wild,
me along with them.
But when Robinson's name
comes over the loudspeaker,
the Negroes jump to their feet,
waving signs like crazy.
You'd think President Roosevelt
came back from the dead.
But they're not the only ones excited.
Everybody wants to see
if Robinson can really play ball in
the big leagues.
Even Pops!

Holy moly, I want to say,
Robinson's okay on first base,
but he's pretty sad at the bat.

After the game he walks over.
"Joey," he says, handing me his shoes,
"seems like you've been missing these."
I shrug.
"Just put them on the pile," I say, hoping he'll leave.
He doesn't.

"You know, Joey," he says, putting a foot on the bench,
"there's people out there who don't
treat me as a man 'cause my skin is black."
His voice is strong, like a line drive.
I don't say nothing.
My eyes are looking at everything but his eyes.
"You know what I've found out about them?"
he asks, almost like I was a friend
he was telling a secret to.

"No," I say.
Normally I'd say "No, sir" to a player.
I couldn't say it now, but I do look up.
I expect his eyes to be angry.
He just looks tired and sort of let down.
"They don't know what a man is," he says.
Then he pulls himself tall and walks away.

I look at the shoes he's left.
If he tells the clubhouse manager
I haven't been doing my job,
I'll get canned.
So I clean those shoes a little better,
but they don't shine.

We head to the home of the New York Giants,
our big rivals.
Robinson gets five hits and his first homer.
It's a humdinger!
Even *I* have to cheer.

Robinson's swamped with fan mail.
I keep loading cards and letters into his slot.
Pops says he'll be gone soon.
He won't be able to hack the big leagues.
But I don't know.
He works hard as anyone
and doesn't ask for no favors.

After the Giants we come back home
for three games against the Phillies.
The day's so cold for Game One,
I have to keep blowing on my fingers to keep warm.
When I hand Robinson his bat,
shouts start coming from the Phillies dugout:
"Why don't you go back to the cotton fields?"
"They're waiting for you in the jungles, black boy."
A bunch of the players aim their bats at him like guns
and shout the *n*-word.

I can't believe it!
This is baseball, for crying out loud.

Robinson just keeps playing.
He hits a single, steals a base, and even scores.
But I can see the ugliness is getting to him.
He makes his first error of the season.

The second game's as rotten as the first,
and our fans are as mad as us.
But then, at the start of the third game,
our second baseman, Eddie Stanky,
stands and roars, "You yellow-bellied cowards,
why don't you yell at somebody
who can answer back?"
Everybody knows Robinson promised
he won't make no trouble—no matter what.
Then another Dodger hollers, "If you guys played
as well as you talked, you'd win some games!"

"Yeah!" I shout like the rest. "Shut your faces!"

Later in the locker room
the players start laughing
and joshing with Jackie
like he's one of the guys.
I guess he is now.

After that, Jackie goes into a hitting slump,
and I wonder,
will he get pulled from the lineup?
On May Day, against the Cubs,
he shoots a line drive to left field.
The slump is broken!
We win the game,
and suddenly we're on top in the league!
I want to shake Jackie's hand or something.
"Congratulations, Mr. Robinson,"
I say as I take his uniform,
and he smiles.
But I feel like he sees
PHILLIES written on my shirt instead of DODGERS.

Jackie isn't living on easy street yet.
Pitchers aim for him—he gets hit six times.
Runners slide into first and try to spike him.
On the road, he can't stay
at the same hotel as the rest of us,
or eat with us, or use the swimming pool.
Letters start coming in so full of hate
the police have to guard him.

If I weren't the batboy,
I don't know if I'd believe it.
Jackie just keeps playing harder and harder.
He goes on a hitting streak,
batting in doubles and homers.
And he steals his way around the diamond.
He even steals home!
The pitchers get so crazy
that they can't pitch for watching Jackie.

By September, we're on top.
Even so, I got a bad feeling I can't shake
or talk to Pops about.
I'm doing my best work for Jackie,
getting the pine tar and rosin for his bats,
delivering his mail, bringing him Chiclets and water.
But I still feel like we're in two different dugouts,
and I'm the one who put us there.

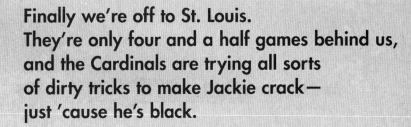

Finally we're off to St. Louis.
They're only four and a half games behind us,
and the Cardinals are trying all sorts
of dirty tricks to make Jackie crack—
just 'cause he's black.

It's the eighth inning of the last game.
One of the Cardinals hits a foul.
Jackie leaps from first to catch it.
Jumping Jehoshaphat, he's going to crash
into the dugout!
Then suddenly Ralph Branca, our pitcher that day,
is in the air like Superman.
As Jackie catches the ball, Ralph catches Jackie!
Holy Joe! A white man holding a black man!
That takes the gobble out of the Cardinals' turkeys!
The batter's out,
and we go on to win the game 8–7.

The Cardinals later lose to the Cubs.

All of Brooklyn is celebrating—
we won the National League Pennant,
and Jackie is the first ever Rookie of the Year!
September 23, 1947,
is Jackie Robinson Day at Ebbets Field.
I get there early and hang out at the dugout
'cause I want to say something to Jackie
before I go sit with Pops.

A bunch of colored boys yell to me from the fence:
"Could you give something to Jackie for us, please?"
A boy about my age hands me a package
and a homemade card.
Jealousy rips through me.
I wish the present was mine.

Reporters are all over him in the locker room.
I get up my courage.
"Mr. Robinson, may I talk to you a minute?"
He gets a what's-this-about? look on his face,
but he excuses himself.
I drag him over to the corner and thrust out the gift,
keeping the card behind my back.
He tears off the wrapping: it's a Louisville Slugger
that's wood-burned on the end—OUR MAN JACK.
His eyes get a softness to them,
like when Pops says good night.

"Thanks, kid," Jackie says. "This means a lot to me."
My mouth gets dry as I look into his dark eyes.
I want to take the credit so bad.
I want him to know that I'm sorry for the shoes and stuff.

But then the words come tumbling out:
"It's not from me, Mr. Robinson. I wish it was."
I'm so nervous I think I'm going to pee.
"It's from some other boys," I add.
"Here's their card."

My eyes go to the floor.
I want to melt into the floor like the witch in *Wizard of Oz.*
"I don't have any bat to give you," I mumble,
"but I want you to know
I got what you mean about what a man is."

I glance up sideways—
something odd ripples across his face.
"Joey," he says, "I look good today
because I've held my cool and we've won the pennant.
But someday I am going to start speaking up and talking back.
And maybe I'll go back into another slump.
What'll you think of me then?"

He's testing me, I think,
and I deserve it.
"Well, you didn't take nothing from me before,"
I say, "and slumps and Dodgers go together—
they don't mean nothing."

A laugh erupts from him at that,
and I can see in his eyes
that I just grew a few feet.
He offers me his hand to shake—
one Dodger to another.
When I grab it,
I feel the tight grip of a friend.

Later I go to find Pops in the stands.
The place is so crowded that it's hard
to see him among all the different-colored faces.
On most everybody's jackets are buttons
saying I'M FOR JACKIE!
I buy one for me and one for Pops.
Still, I'm not sure he'll wear his.

But when I say, "Here, Pops,"
he puts it right on.
"Joey, my boy," he says,
"someday you'll be boasting to your kids
that you were his batboy.
That man's earned his place in history."

When Jackie and his family walk out
on the field, we all go nuts,
but I feel like a Grand Slam hitter.
Dem bums, the Dodgers, are *some* team,
and . . .

WE'RE ALL ON IT!

Afterword

The Dodgers lost the 1947 World Series to the New York Yankees, but it was one of the most exciting series that ever was, with the end score of four games to three.

With that 1947 season, Jack Roosevelt Robinson became the very first African American to play baseball in America's Major Leagues since the late 1800s.

Though few remember it, Jackie also helped pioneer a place for black players in basketball. In November and December of 1946, Robinson played with the Los Angeles Red Devils, a team seeking admission to the National Basketball League. He was one of five men to be the first African Americans to play in the NBL. But Robinson had to choose between basketball and baseball, and his choice is history.

Jackie earned the very first Rookie of the Year Award in baseball by playing better than his teammates in several areas: scoring runs (125), stealing bases (28—a league high), bunting, and running bases. He also shared the honor for the most doubles and home runs hit, and ended the 1947 season with a .297 batting average.

With his face on *Time* magazine, Jackie Robinson was named the most popular man in the United States, second only to the singer Bing Crosby.

But this did not end the racism that Robinson and others faced. For the next ten years in baseball, Jackie lived through insults, injuries, and threats, especially after he began to speak about unfair practices against black people. He said, "I learned that as long as I appeared to ignore insult and injury, I was a martyred hero to a lot of people who seemed to have sympathy for the underdog. But the minute I began to answer, to argue, to protest . . . I became a swellhead, a wise guy, an 'uppity' nigger. When a white guy did it, he had spirit. When a black man did it, he was 'ungrateful', 'an upstart', 'a sorehead'."

Jackie's work for equality did not harm his playing. He continued to set records in stolen bases, in second-base fielding, and second-baseman double plays (he'd moved from first base back to second base—his favored position). His lifetime batting average in the Major Leagues was .311, and he was voted Most Valuable Player in 1949.

He also worked with youth of all races and wrote a children's book called *Jackie Robinson's Little League Baseball Book*. He became a vice president of a national company, helped found an African-American bank in Harlem, and pushed tirelessly for equal opportunities and an end to racism.

In 1962 Jackie Robinson was inducted into the Baseball Hall of Fame. He thanked three people especially: his mother, Mallie McGriff Robinson (who was the daughter of slaves); his wife and closest friend, Rachel Isum Robinson; and Branch Rickey Sr., the owner of the Brooklyn Dodgers.

In 1972, shortly before his death, Jackie was honored at the twenty-fifth anniversary of his entry into the Major Leagues. "I am extremely proud and pleased," he stated. "But I'm going to be tremendously more pleased and more proud when I look at that third-base coaching line one day and see a black face managing in baseball."

Note from the Author

Jackie Robinson *may* have had a batboy like Joey. We don't know. So Joey, and the conversations between him and Jackie, are all imagined. I thank Jackie's wife, Rachel, for checking that Jackie's comments in this story fit who Jackie really was.

However, everything that Joey observes and overhears about Jackie's first year in baseball is factually true: from his teammates not wanting to play with him during spring training; to the nasty game with the Phillies and Jackie's teammate's change of heart; to the death threats and the hate mail and the love of the fans; to the accounts of the games, Jackie Robinson Day, and the Rookie of the Year Award. These descriptions and quotations are all based on historical accounts.